GREAT
EXPECTATIONS

Written by **Charles Dickens**
Illustrations by **Pipi Sposito**

스푼북

Pip Meets a Convict

This story is about Philip Pirrip. Everyone called him Pip. He couldn't remember his mother and father because they died when he was very young.

MRS JOE

Pip's sister, who was twenty years older, took on the task of bringing up young Pip. She was married to Joe Gargery, a strong, kind man with fair, curly hair and blue eyes. Joe was a blacksmith in the village, which lay on the flat and marshy Thames estuary, not too far from the sea.

JOE GARGERY

Joe was big and strong, but he was a little frightened of his wife. Pip was frightened of her too.

Mrs Joe – that's what everyone called her – was quick to fight with both Pip and Joe. She fought with words, and sometimes even with a cane.

Though Pip couldn't remember
his parents, sometimes he went to
the churchyard and gazed at their
gravestones.

Pip was in the churchyard
one Christmas Eve. The day was

growing darker and he shivered as
the wind rushed in from the river.
He was feeling sorry for himself
and began to cry.

'Hold your noise!' cried a terrible voice.

A huge man sprang up from among the gravestones. He was dressed in ragged grey clothes. He was wet and muddy, and shivering. Worst of all, he had an iron chain locking his ankles together.

'What's your name, boy?'

'Pip, sir.'

'Where do you live?'

His hand trembling, the boy pointed to his village about a mile off.

'Where's your mother and father?' growled the man.

'There,' said Pip, nodding towards the tombstones. 'I live with my sister, Mrs Joe. She's married to Joe Gargery, the blacksmith.'

'Blacksmith, eh?' said the man, looking at the chain around his ankles. He stretched out his large hands and squeezed Pip hard by the cheeks. 'Here's what you're going to do, boy. Go home and bring me back some food and a file tomorrow morning. If you don't – I might just eat you instead, starting with these fat cheeks of yours.'

Pip ran home in terror. His sister was on the rampage and started shouting at him. She stamped her foot, shook her fist and screeched questions about what mischief he had been up to.

Later, during tea, Pip managed to hide a slice of bread and butter for the grey man on the marshes. In the distance, they heard the booming sound of a cannon being fired. Joe said it came from the

prison-ship moored in the estuary.
It meant that a prisoner, a convict,
had escaped.

Pip hardly slept that night. Very
early on Christmas morning, he
crept downstairs and took some
cheese, a little brandy in a bottle
and a beautiful round pork pie from
his sister's pantry.

He ran through the misty morning until he found the grey man. Seizing the food and drink, the man gulped it down like a starving dog.

Pip plucked up the courage to say, 'I am glad you enjoyed it.'

In reply, the man made a strange clicking sound in his throat. He demanded the file taken from Joe's workshop, then seemed to forget about the boy. When Pip left, the man was filing away furiously at the chain around his legs.

Mrs Joe had guests for Christmas dinner. One of them was Mr Pumblechook, Joe's uncle, who had a mouth like a fish. He and the other grown-ups lectured Pip about how grateful he should be to his sister for bringing him up.

Worse followed when Mrs Joe went to fetch the pork pie from the pantry. Pip knew the pork pie had been swallowed almost in one gulp by the man on the marshes. At any moment his sister would return empty-handed and on the rampage.

Pip thought it best not to be there when this happened. He broke away from the dinner table and ran to the front door …

straight into a group of soldiers.

One of them, a sergeant, was holding a pair of handcuffs.

Thankfully, they were not looking for a pork-pie thief, but for the escaped convict from the prison-ship.

Everyone was excited at the prospect of hunting down a fugitive. Only kind-hearted Joe whispered to Pip that he hoped the prisoner would not be found. Pip hoped so too.

Joe and Pip set off with the soldiers and a handful of people from the village. It was cold and dreary, and Joe carried the boy on his back over banks and across ditches. There was a sudden cry of alarm to their right. It didn't come from the soldiers. They headed towards the sound.

A man was floundering in a patch of swampy ground, about to be sucked under. It was dark now, but even without seeing him clearly Pip knew that it was the man in grey. Three soldiers dragged him from the muddy bog.

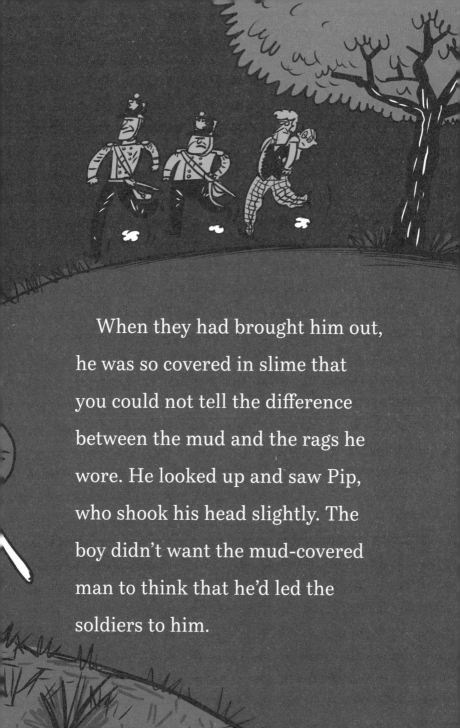

When they had brought him out, he was so covered in slime that you could not tell the difference between the mud and the rags he wore. He looked up and saw Pip, who shook his head slightly. The boy didn't want the mud-covered man to think that he'd led the soldiers to him.

'We've got you now, Abel Magwitch,' said the sergeant.

'I want to say something, in case anyone else gets the blame,' said the prisoner. 'I broke into a blacksmith's close by. I stole a file and a pork pie.'

'You are welcome to the pork pie,' said Joe. 'Whatever you've done, we wouldn't have you starve to death.'

The convict said nothing, but again came that strange clicking sound from his throat. It was as if no one had ever said a kind word to him before.

The sergeant and the soldiers led him away.

'What will happen to him, Joe?' Pip whispered.

'It'll be back to the prison-ship for Mr Magwitch,' said Joe. 'And then he'll be taken to Australia.'

'Australia? Where's that?'

'Not sure, Pip. A long way off, though.'

Pip fell asleep as Joe carried him home on his back.

Satis House

Pip never really thought about what he was going to do in his life. The reason he never thought about it was because he already knew. He was going to be a blacksmith like Joe. Pip had already started helping Joe in the smithy.

Things quickly changed when Mr Pumblechook announced that Pip had been invited to meet a rich lady. She lived in the market town nearby. Her name was Miss Havisham and she wanted a little boy to go and play at her grand house.

Mrs Joe said this was a fine thing. Mr Pumblechook said this was a fine thing. No one asked Pip what he thought. He was washed and scrubbed and dressed up in his smartest clothes. Then Mr Pumblechook drove him in his carriage to Miss Havisham's house. It had a strange name: Satis House. Through a fence of iron bars Pip could see a courtyard. All the windows on the ground floor had iron bars on, too.

Mr Pumblechook rang a bell by the gate. After a while, a young girl strolled across the courtyard holding a bunch of keys. She let Pip in, but told Mr Pumblechook he wasn't wanted by Miss Havisham. At this news, Mr Pumblechook's mouth looked more fish-like than ever.

The girl said almost nothing, apart from telling Pip to hurry up. She called him "boy", even though they were about the same age. But she was so beautiful and confident that she seemed much, much older.

Inside the house, it was dark. The girl picked up a burning candle and they weaved their way through a maze of passages until they came to a door.

'Go in,' she said.

'After you, miss.'

'Don't be ridiculous, boy. I am not going in.'

Half afraid, Pip knocked on
the door and was told to enter.
The room was large and well-
lit with candles. Heavy curtains
covered the windows. In an
armchair sat the strangest lady Pip
had ever seen. A white veil dangled
from her white hair. She was
dressed all in white. Jewels sparkled
on her neck and hands.

'You are the boy sent by
Pumblechook?'

'Yes, ma'am. I am Pip.'

'Come closer,' she demanded.

As he drew near, Pip saw that
her long white dress was faded and
yellow with age.

'How old are you, Pip?'

'Eight, ma'am.'

'I have not seen the light of the
sun since you were born, Pip.'

Since Pip didn't know what to
say, he said nothing. Then Miss
Havisham told him to summon
"Estella". Very uncertain, Pip went
to the door and called 'Estella!' into
the dark corridor. He was pleased
to see the beautiful young girl arrive
back, holding her candle.

Miss Havisham wanted to watch Estella and Pip play cards together. The only game he knew was a simple one called Beggar My Neighbour. Estella beat him at several games. She didn't smile once in all the time they played. She made rude remarks about Pip's clumsy hands.

Finally, Pip was allowed to go home, but told to come back again in a few days. Estella almost pushed him out of the iron front gate and then locked it firmly. Pip was pleased to leave, but sad, too. It was nice to have someone to play with.

Back home, Mrs Joe and Mr Pumblechook peppered Pip with questions about Miss Havisham and Satis House. Pip made up a story about how Miss Havisham was tall and sat on a velvet couch. From the way Mr Pumblechook

nodded in agreement, it was
obvious he'd never been inside
Satis House. Pip felt a little guilty
about telling lies in front of Joe.

A Mysterious Benefactor

This was the start of many visits to Miss Havisham's. Pip didn't enjoy them, though he was always glad to see Estella. And Estella was always glad to be rude to him. She often remarked on how "common and coarse" he was.

Pip found out that Miss Havisham had adopted Estella, and she liked to watch them play together.

There were sometimes other visitors to Satis House. These were distant members of Miss Havisham's family. Once, Pip got into a fight with a tall, pale boy. He didn't start it, but he won. Estella was secretly watching, and she allowed Pip to kiss her afterwards. It never happened again; the fight or the kiss.

Pip's visits went on for several years, until the time came for him to learn Joe's trade as a blacksmith. The apprenticeship was drawn up properly and legally in front of a magistrate in the nearby market town. It meant that the young man's time with Miss Havisham – and Estella – was at an end.

Estella was moving to London to become a lady. Meanwhile, Pip was going to stay in the village and become a blacksmith, just like Joe. Once, Pip would have loved nothing better than to be like Joe: an honest skilful worker. But his regular visits to the grand house had made him want more than that. He had no choice, though. What else could he do?

In front of him stretched a life of working in the heat and sweat of the blacksmith's forge. There was more work to be done at home now, too. Mrs Joe had been seriously injured. Now she sat quiet, tame and incapable in a corner. No more rampaging. A girl from the village called Biddy came to help Pip and Joe look after her.

Then, one day, something happened to change everything.

By now, Pip was in the habit of going to the village pub, The Three Jolly Bargemen. One Saturday night, he and Joe were there with some others when a strange man came in. He watched them from his seat and kept biting his finger as if it were a tasty snack. Then he stuck out that finger like an accusation.

'I believe,' he said, 'there is a
blacksmith by the name of Joe
Gargery among you.'

'That's me,' said Joe.

'You have an apprentice known
as Pip?'

'That is I,' said Pip.

The stranger didn't recognise Pip, but Pip remembered him. He had passed him once on the stairs at Miss Havisham's, a long time ago. He had a large head and bushy eyebrows. Pip had thought he must be a member of Miss Havisham's family.

But no. It turned out that he was a lawyer from London. His name was Jaggers, and he wanted to speak to Joe and Pip privately. The best place to do this was in their parlour at home. It was hardly ever used after Mrs Joe's accident.

Mr Jaggers sat down at their parlour table and said, 'Mr Pip, you have a benefactor. Do you understand what that means?'

Joe's and Pip's blank faces showed that they did not.

'A benefactor,' went on Mr Jaggers in his deep voice, 'is a person who wants to do something good for you, and who has the means to do it. That is to say, the person in question has money. Your benefactor, Mr Pip, has great expectations for you and wishes you to go to London.'

'Why?' said Pip, shocked. 'What am I going to do in London?'

'You will learn how to be a gentleman, and gentlemen do not have to do anything.'

'Who is this kind benefactor?' Pip asked, though he already knew.

It had to be Miss Havisham! She wanted him to become a gentleman so that he could marry Estella!

'I cannot say.' Mr Jaggers replied. 'Your benefactor wants to remain unknown until the day he – or she – chooses to reveal their identity.'

There was plenty more to listen to and be amazed by. Meanwhile, Joe hardly said a word.

OFF TO LONDON

Within a week, Pip said his goodbyes to Joe, Mrs Joe, Biddy and Mr Pumblechook. Now that he was starting on the road to becoming a gentleman, they behaved differently towards him. It was almost as if he were a stranger.

That morning, carrying a little suitcase and quite alone, Pip caught the coach to London.

First Pip called at Mr Jaggers' office. The lawyer was Pip's guardian. He would provide a monthly allowance of money until Pip's benefactor chose to appear.

'Welcome, Mr Pip,' said the lawyer. 'What do you think of London?'

'It is very big,' Pip said, 'and – and busier and dirtier than I expected.'

Pip hesitated to say this because he thought it might be rude. Mr Jaggers simply laughed. He explained that Pip was to live with a young gentleman called Herbert Pocket. He would be taught about books and manners by Herbert's father, Mr Matthew Pocket. The Pockets were all distant cousins to Miss Havisham.

When Herbert and Pip met, they gazed at each other in surprise. He was grown up now

of course, but Herbert was the
same tall, pale boy Pip had fought
at Miss Havisham's. But Herbert
didn't bear Pip any grudge. In fact,
he was very friendly.

Herbert explained the reason why Miss Havisham stayed indoors and always wore the same old white dress. He said that years ago she was supposed to marry a man. But on the morning of the wedding, he wrote to her breaking off the marriage.

'Did you ever notice the clock in her room?' said Herbert.

'Yes, it was stopped at twenty to nine,' said Pip.

'That is the time she received the letter. Everything froze in time at that moment. The dress she wears is her wedding dress.'

Herbert said that Miss Havisham had trained Estella to be cold and to treat people, especially men, as cruelly as Miss Havisham herself had been treated. Estella was trained to break men's hearts.

Joe came to visit Pip at his lodgings in London. Pip introduced him to Herbert, who was very gracious. But Pip was embarrassed by Joe, even though the village blacksmith had dressed in his Sunday best. Joe even called him 'Sir' when he always used to say 'Pip'.

Sometimes Pip saw Estella, too. She had grown into a beautiful lady. She was no longer rude to him. The two were almost friends, though she never returned his smiles.

Pip believed that his benefactor was Miss Havisham. If she wanted him to become a gentleman, she must have changed her mind about wanting Estella to break men's hearts. Maybe Estella wouldn't break Pip's heart, at least.

Pip went back to his old village a few times, including for the funeral when his sister, Mrs Joe, died. But he no longer belonged there.

Things went on like this for some years. In London, Pip learnt to dress better, to behave better, to speak French, and to ride a horse. Everything a gentleman should do.

He often spent more money than he should. Mr Jaggers, who provided his allowance, would wag his bitten finger and tell him to stop spending so much. Then Pip would ask him when the identity

of his benefactor would be revealed.
He already knew who she was of
course.

'You'll know in good time, Mr
Pip,' was all Mr Jaggers would say.

The time finally came.

A Surprise Visitor

It was a dark and stormy night. Herbert, with whom Pip still shared lodgings, was away. Their rooms were at the top of an old house near the river. The wind shook the windows and blew the smoke from the fireplace back down the chimney.

Suddenly, Pip heard the stumble of a footstep downstairs. He took the lamp and went out onto the landing. The stairway lights had blown out.

'Which floor do you want?' Pip
called.

'The top,' said a deep voice.

The man climbed up the stairs. He
wore a rough coat. Long. iron-grey
hair flowed from beneath his hat.

'What do you want?' said Pip.

'You, Mr Pip. I wish to come in.'

From the look on the man's face as the lamplight fell across it, he seemed pleased to see Pip. But Pip did not know him.

Once inside, the man shrugged off his coat and stood near the fire. The way he held his large brown hands out to the heat suddenly made Pip realise who he was.

The man saw the recognition on Pip's face.

'Yes, it's me! Abel Magwitch. From the prison-ship. The man on the marshes that you helped by bringing food and a file to when you was a lad.'

Pip stepped back in horror.

'Weren't you taken to Australia?' he gasped.

Many prisoners, men and women, were transported by boat to serve prison time on the other side of the world, in Australia. There they could eventually be

freed, but they would never be allowed to return to England.

Magwitch told Pip that he'd served time for his crimes. Once free, he had done well and made money as a sheep-farmer in Australia. Lots of money.

'If I'm caught back in England, I'm done for,' said Magwitch. 'But it was worth it to see what a fine gentleman my boy has become. Look, you're wearing better clothes than me. And is that a gold ring on your finger, my boy?'

Pip nodded. He had a terrible suspicion what was coming next.

'Who paid for them clothes and ring, Mr Pip?'

'It was you!' exclaimed Pip. 'You are my benefactor.'

'That's the lawyer's word which Jaggers uses. I'd rather say I'm a friend to you, Mr Pip. I'm like your second father. You helped me once. And I've been helping you ever since.'

That night Magwitch slept in Herbert's room. Pip couldn't sleep at all. The rain and wind drummed heavily against his windows.

He asked himself again and again: how could he have been so stupid?

Miss Havisham had never been Pip's benefactor. Yes, Mr Jaggers was her lawyer, but he was also Magwitch's lawyer.

So Miss Havisham had never intended for Pip to marry Estella. Everything Pip had in his new life as a gentleman had come from a criminal. He felt ashamed.

These thoughts were chased away
by the knowledge that Magwitch's
life would be over if he were caught.
He had risked not just his freedom
but his life to see Pip.

Pip was in Magwitch's debt, and had to help him get to safety. He needed to get him out of the country before he was captured.

Herbert returned the next day and Pip spilled all these secrets to him. Good friend that he was, Herbert agreed to help in Magwitch's escape.

This was urgent, for Magwitch believed that he might already have been spotted on his return to London.

The only way was to get Magwitch on board a steamboat, bound for somewhere far away. Magwitch could not risk boarding in London itself. Instead they planned to row downriver to a remote place on the Thames estuary. They would stay there overnight and catch a passing boat to Holland or Germany.

While they were planning, there was a tragedy. Satis House burnt to the ground and Miss Havisham died in the fire.

The place where Pip had first fallen in love with Estella was gone, taking with it any remaining hope that Estella would return that love. But Pip had no time to feel sorry for for himself. He and Herbert had to get Abel Magwitch safely out of England.

Magwitch's Escape

Magwitch was the calmest
of them all when they
embarked on the first
stage of the escape.
Herbert and Pip pulled
at the oars, but he sat
smoking his pipe in the

stern of the little rowing boat as if they were on a pleasure trip.

Pip was no longer frightened of Magwitch or ashamed of the connection between them. Abel Magwitch had only tried to do good by him, and now he would do good by Abel Magwitch.

They stayed overnight at a dingy public house called The Ship, whose sign squeaked in the wind. The next day was bright and clear. They waited

at the entrance to a creek, watching

for the smudge of smoke from the

approaching steamboat.

There it was! As fast as they

could, Herbert and Pip steered

the little boat out into the river.
They aimed to draw alongside the
steamboat, whose paddles beat
through the water. On the side it
said "HAMBURG". This steamboat
would take Abel Magwitch to
Germany.

At the same moment that they
reached the open river, a large

rowing boat filled with policemen
pulled out from the river bank. It
steered towards them. The police's
boat was faster.

Pip's boat continued frantically
on its path and the police followed.
Just as the three of them reached
the steamboat, the police rammed
them with their bow. Abel had been
crouching in the stern.

Now he was thrown overboard. Pip was afraid that he had been struck by the steamboat's paddles and pushed under. But as the Hamburg steamer thudded by, he saw a body floating in the water.

The police dragged Abel out. He was still alive, but only just. Nevertheless, they put him in handcuffs.

Pip was allowed to go back with them in the police boat, while Herbert returned to the shore.

Abel Magwitch could barely speak. 'You can leave me now, my

boy,' he said. His voice was so faint that Pip had to bend close to hear.

'Never,' said Pip. 'I will never leave you. I will be as true to you as you have been to me.'

There came that strange clicking sound in his throat that Pip remembered from long ago.

Pip Returns to Satis House

There is no need to make a longer story of it. Abel Magwitch died in the prison hospital. Pip was with him until the end.

Abel never knew that his plan of making Pip into a gentleman had failed. All of

Magwitch's money was confiscated because he had broken the law by returning to England. Pip was left with nothing. But Abel Magwitch had changed Pip in other ways. Changed him for the better, perhaps.

Pip returned to the little village where he was brought up. There

he discovered that Joe and Biddy
had married. He was glad for
them.

After that, Pip went to Satis
House. It was a ruin because of the
fire. Only the bare stumps of walls
and blackened floors remained.

There was a figure wandering
in the ruins, just like him. It was

Estella, tall and elegant. Pip had only ever known her to be cold and emotionless. Now her sadness was clear in the way she moved.

Pip picked his way through the remains of Miss Havisham's old house.

'Estella,' he said.

'Pip?' Estella said. 'Is that you?'

'Yes. It's me.'

'Good.'

Though it was growing dark, Pip could see her clearly now.

She was smiling.

Charles Dickens

Charles Dickens was born in Portsmouth in 1812. Like many of the characters he wrote about, his family were poor and his childhood was difficult. As an adult, he became known around the world for his books. He is remembered as one of the most important writers of his time.

Illustrations by
Pipi Sposito

Pipi Sposito was born in Buenos Aires. He's always been painting. As a child, he enjoyed making figures out of building clay, and when he was older, he started designing for humor magazines. He was surrounded by the original paintings of many experimental artists, and he painted various styles out of curiosity. His illustrated books include 《A Christmas Carol》《A Tale of Two Cities》《Great Expectations》《Oliver Twist》.

GREAT EXPECTATIONS

초판 1쇄 발행 2023년 6월 27일

글 찰스 디킨스 ｜ 그림 피피 스포지토

ISBN 979-11-6581-433-5 (74840)
ISBN 979-11-6581-418-2 (세트)

＊잘못 만들어진 책은 구입하신 곳에서 바꾸어 드립니다.

발행처 주식회사 스푼북 ｜ **발행인** 박상희 ｜ **총괄** 김남원
편집 김선영·박선정·김선혜·권새미 ｜ **디자인** 조혜진·김광휘 ｜ **마케팅** 손준연·이성호·구혜지
출판신고 2016년 11월 15일 제2017-000267호
주소 (03993) 서울시 마포구 월드컵북로 6길 88-7 ky21빌딩 2층
전화 02-6357-0050(편집) 02-6357-0051(마케팅)
팩스 02-6357-0052 ｜ 전자우편 book@spoonbook.co.kr